SLOBCAT

Paul Geraghty

RED FOX

For Harriet and the Moppets

A Red Fox Book

Published by Random House Children's Books
61-63 Uxbridge Road, London W5 5SA

A division of Random House UK Ltd
London Melbourne Sydney Auckland
Johannesburg and agencies throughout the world

First published by Hutchinson Children's Books 1991

Red Fox edition 1993

10

RANDOM HOUSE UK Limited Reg. No. 954009
www.rbooks.co.uk

Printed in Hong Kong

ISBN 978 0 09 971690 7

Slobcat is our cat.
He does nothing but lie
about and sleep.

Heaven knows what
he does when we're
not there.

But when we get home he's still sleeping. That's why we call him Slobcat.

When it's his dinner time,
he's nowhere to be seen...

...and when we *do* find him,
he's even too lazy to eat.

I don't know *where* he goes
when we put him out...

…but he often comes back soaking wet because he's too lazy to shelter from the rain.

He spends so much
time inside...

…that he ends up getting in the way!

Last week Mum saw a
mouse, so Dad put
out a trap...

...because Slobcat
isn't interested
in chasing mice.

All *he's* interested in is lying about in the sun.

Luckily,
we don't have rats...

…because if we did,
Dad says we'd have to
get a proper cat.

Some people have
dangerous animals
in their gardens.

But for some reason,
they don't seem to
come into ours.

It's strange because the *little* creatures don't seem afraid.

Sometimes, when we're asleep, there are burglars about.

Thank goodness we have Brutus to frighten them off…

...because Slobcat couldn't frighten a flea!

People say that all cats have a secret
life that we don't know about…

...but I'm sure Slobcat's
much too lazy for that!